Elpidio's Chronicle: A Remarkable Odyssey

by

Gerard Adrian Menezes

"Elpidio's Chronicle: A Remarkable Odyssey" published through Young Author Academy.

Young Author Academy FZCO
Dubai, United Arab Emirates

www.youngauthoracademy.com

ISBN: 9798869702456

Printed by Amazon Direct Publishing.

To my mother
for encouraging me to
pen my creative thoughts
into this book of adventure.

- Chapter One -

It was a serene Thursday morning on the third last day in 2022 - a year of a number that is a multiple of three - usually lucky for an average thirteen-year-old, whose birthday passed about three days ago.

My name is Elpidio Rana. One of my favourite pastimes is playing Minecraft with my friends while living a normal life in Harmonville, Tenoria. Our house is worth a fortune and is secluded from the rest of Glenville Estates and downtown Harmonville.

One day, a mysterious person started to continuously knock creepily on the door of our house. As my mom, Mrs. Rana, opened the white wooden old-school-style front door, it seemed like I was kind of overreacting about it being a serial killer trying to target us or something. It appeared to be my friends, the twins, Marcus, and Mark's family coming for dinner.

There was the usual greeting that was common between our families, which was, 'Hi! Hello!'... that kind of stuff, "Yeah, yeah."

Mr. and Mrs. Benson entered our spotless home, which was adorned with numerous decorations and artwork, collected from travels over the years.

Mr. and Mrs. Benson had a skin tone that matched chocolate, as did Mark and Marcus (they were fifteen already).

Mrs. Benson took out her thin glasses from her designer purse and put them on. Mark and Marcus then both came out in a red t-shirt and black tracksuit pants. My mom told me to head upstairs to my room with Marcus and Mark.

As we headed upstairs to the second floor, I was reminded of the usual eerie experience I have when I walk upstairs because, in horror movies like 'The Conjuring' or 'Insidious', there are multiple demons - or ghosts - trying to get inside your soul.

We reached the second floor, then passed my parents' bedroom, we continued past my annoying big sister's room, and finally, at the end of the corridor, we reached my room. The door was brown (unlike the other doors of the bathrooms and bedrooms on the second floor, which are all white).

We entered my room, which was filled with blue walls and a huge study desk that held at least fifty books. It looks kind of messy now, but it's okay. I switched on the 55-inch TV and with the black rectangular remote firmly held in my hand, I pressed the 'HDMI 5' button, which was the setting I use to play on my PS5.

YESS! After what seemed like an eternity, the game finally loaded. Usually, we would play Minecraft when we got together; however, today we decided to play NBA 2K23 for a change. It was a lot of fun playing together for hours in what felt like only fifteen minutes.

After a few moments, it was... precisely midnight. We finished our scrumptious dinner, which my mom toiled to make since morning, preparing for this lovely evening. It was a wonderful time spent with my friends; it was very late at night, therefore Mark and Marcus had to head back home. It was a pleasure to host Mr. and Mrs. Benson at our place.

Mr. and Mrs. Benson started saying their goodbyes ushering Mark and Marcus to follow. Mr. Benson opened the door and they walked out with Marcus and Mark, waving goodbye to us as they left our home. My mom and I thanked them for coming over and wished them a good night.

As my mom walked towards the door and closed it, she commanded me to brush my teeth and go to bed. I headed upstairs, ignoring that eerie feeling again, and went into my room. I turned left into the precisely seven-foot passageway that led to my bathroom garnished with a row of coat hangers on my right, hanging on the rack in my wardrobe. I opened the white oak door to my bathroom, which had light grey ceramic mosaic tiles on the floor and walls, and then entered the shower cubicle that stood straight off the entrance.

After a long evening of finishing my chores, I turned off my nightlight and retired to bed.

- Chapter Two -

It was 06:59 on my digital alarm clock that sat on my nightstand bellowed to wake me. I woke up with a roaring yawn that resembled a wolf and gently rubbed my eyes to the sound of annoying rap music, blaring from the neighbouring house. I got so fussed to hear a rap this early in the day due to the fact that it always disturbed my sleep awfully. I felt so irritated to start my day on a bad note.

I looked at the calendar in my room, checking the date - as I almost always do - today was December 30, 2022, which meant that my luck would not last forever. My luck usually lasts in years where the numbers are multiples of 3 (i.e., 2016, 2019, 2022, 2025, etc.). This also meant that my luck would last only until tomorrow.

I'm doomed... My lucky days would not last long. I wondered what was in store for me now. I could only hope for the best; it cannot be too bad, surely.

My Calendar:

January 2023

Monday	Tuesday	Wednesday	Thursday	Friday	Saturday	Sunday
26	27	28	29	30	31	1
2	3	4	5	6	7	8
9	10	11	12	13	14	15
16	17	18	19	20	21	22
23	24	25	26	27	28	29
30	31					

I just realised.... School starts in three days! Sheesh! This meant that the second day of 2023 would be unlucky. Why? Because I have not touched the sky and I was not born in the month of July. Just kidding! I was just being too cringe.

Fortunately, the last day of the year and New Year's went well, and I had an excellent semester break but now, it was time to get ready for school, which starts tomorrow.

- Chapter Three -

The day finally arrived. It was the beginning of a new school semester after a wonderful three-week semester break. I got up as usual and strapped my yellow school bag to my back, as Mom wished me luck for my first day. I was excited and was looking forward to this brand-new semester.

I dashed out the door excitedly and left for school. I usually took the sidewalk to school. I walked over to the bus stop at Glenville Estates 28th Street and boarded the grey Mercedes Benz eCitaro bus, which always travelled in the direction of Heavensdale. The Harmonville Central Auditorium, which was seventeen stops from Heavensdale and two stops from my house, was where I normally got off for school.

Eight minutes passed and the bus reached my destination. I got off the bus and walked over the crossing to my school, Harmonville Central High.

Harmonville Central High was a four-storey yellow-reddish building. It was painted during the winter break, which was why I could still smell the paint. The odour was getting on my nerves. I always disliked the smell of paint because it made me feel nauseated. Unfortunately, my best friend Marcus likes it, which irritated me the most about him.

I walked into school and looked at the timetable for grade 9E (the class I am in this year), the timetable read, "Please go to the 3rd Floor, (Room 315) for Geography."

The first class was set to begin at 8 a.m. I looked at my navy blue Apple Watch Series 8 to confirm if I was on time for class. I then took the stairs to the third floor, where my geography class was to be. I walked through the beige wooden-coloured doorway into my classroom.

Mr. Abdulaziz, my teacher, greeted me with a wave and welcomed me into the classroom. I took my seat, which was in the far back, left-centre of the classroom. Eamon was on my left, and Patrik was on my right.

Today appeared to be a long day, especially after a very enjoyable vacation; the first day of school after a semester break turned out to be the longest. It was about 14:40, we were in the middle of an intriguing history lesson, and suddenly, I heard gunshots coming from inside the school, followed by the sight of armed men with rifles shooting at anyone they could spot from the far corner.

I was flabbergasted by the terrifying sounds and cries. Before I could even react, I saw teachers and students going haywire. They were so fearful of being hit, that they could not even think about where they were going. I continued to hear deafening gunshots, which grew louder as time passed.

Fearfully, I decided to look for Marcus as tears streamed down my cheeks and my heart pounded like a thud, but I couldn't, the armed men were everywhere, and I did not want to get shot. I did not want to die.

Students screamed, teachers sobbed, and blood began to splash and stain the freshly painted interior walls of the school. Everything was in complete disarray, and the school was filled with commotion, fear and panic. We were all worried about our safety, including myself.

'I do not want to die, I want to live,' I began to think, 'I just hope we can all get out of here safely.'

- Chapter Four -

After a couple of hours standing in the same place, I managed to grab an opportunity to escape the field of view of the gunmen and instantly ran to the boy's restroom in order to hide from the shootings.

I ran into one of the cubicles in the boys' restroom and shut the door. I sat on the toilet seat, crouched on the cover in fear, holding both my knees, and waited until the gunshots were over. After two hours, the gunshots subsided. Some time later, Patrik also managed to sneak into the cubicle adjacent to mine. I heard the door creak, and then it stopped, making a single sound, and then maintained pin-drop silence.

About half an hour passed by, and I then heard a knock on the cubicle door, which I had locked earlier. I waited for a couple of seconds in order to make sure that it was not a gunman. The anonymous person knocked on the door again and then said, "Don't worry, child, I am a police officer. I won't harm you."

This convinced me enough that the coast was clear, so I unlocked the door. After seeing the policeman, I was extremely relieved and I let him escort me out of the cubicle. I was glad to see Patrik also being led out safely by the same police officer. We were then escorted safely down the stairs along with several other children and staff into an open area of the school.

As we were being ushered out of the building, I noticed several other police officers shepherding other students and faculty. When we were escorted into the open, I saw a few ambulances carrying seriously injured people as well as police cars with the gunmen inside them and three policemen. About twelve buses were waiting to take us home safely.

After a horrendous experience, I finally reached home, and I was extremely happy to see my mom, who was eagerly waiting for my arrival. She hugged me tightly and frantically asked if I was okay, or if I was hurt anywhere. I reassured her that I was okay and not hurt, and she was only relieved after listening and knowing my responses. I could not have felt safer anywhere else than in my mother's loving arms.

January 2nd, 2023, was the wretchedest day of my life.

- Chapter Five -

I returned to my room, still reeling from the events of the day. Later, Mom came to my room to check on me. She looked at me and knew I was still in trauma and needed her to comfort me; hence, she decided to sleep with me tonight, knowing I would probably have nightmares and possibly stay awake all night. I then got into bed and switched the light off. I somehow managed to get some sleep, despite being petrified about the day's - soon to be yesterday's - tragedy.

The next day, when I woke up, I did not find Mom next to me, and I checked my alarm clock; it read 1:58 p.m. Only then did I realise that I had slept the entire morning through to the afternoon.

It was a new day for me to start afresh, by braving the pain from yesterday's tragedy and moving on.

I walked down to the kitchen hoping to find Mom, and to my surprise, I found her eating at the dining table with Andrea, my older sister.

Andrea was supposed to be at university, and she was due to return on Friday, but there was a change of plans after she heard of the school tragedy. She came home sooner for my moral support, despite all the quarrels we had all the time.

Mom then told me that she received an email from the principal saying that we were to have three weeks off as there were ongoing renovations due to the damages sustained at the school.

- Chapter Six -

After hearing the news about the holidays, I started to develop mixed feelings about everything that was going on. I wasn't sure how these days would pass. Yesterday's tragedy still lingered in my mind deeply. That's when Mom broke the news that we would travel to Muscat after three days. Upon hearing that, I jumped with joy.

I almost forgot to mention that Muscat International Airport was my favourite airport in the entire world, which added to my excitement for the trip.

Andrea and I were looking forward to our trip. I had forgotten about the tragedy and was preparing for our upcoming trip. I then called

Patrik and Marcus, and after checking in on them, I told them I was going to Muscat for the holidays. I was relieved to hear that they were doing well despite the tragedy that had also affected them.

For the trip, we would need a lot of supplies for a high-adventure type of vacation, so Mom told Andrea and me to start packing accordingly.

- Chapter Seven -

We were so busy packing our bags, sorting things, and making our plans for our trip that we didn't realise how the three days had passed in a jiffy.

The day has come! Hooray! It was finally the day we would leave for our trip. We were all so excited and couldn't wait to get on the plane.

We headed out of our house hurriedly into the taxi and headed towards the airport. It was a long way to the airport so I kind of slept during the taxi ride, and I remember nothing much at all about the journey.

After we reached the airport, we completed the necessary checking formalities before we boarded the Boeing 777 aircraft of FlyWorld airline at Gate 2A. We walked through the airbridge and onto the flight.

Speaking of planes and aviation, I always wanted to become a pilot, a dream I'd had since the age of three. I really enjoy online flight simulators and imagine myself often soaring high in the sky.

I then got into the seat of the aircraft. I fell asleep the instant I sat down in my seat. I had forgotten to buckle my seatbelt and put a blanket over it. A few minutes later, an air hostess woke me up to tell me to do this. Before takeoff, I somehow got to scroll through my phone, and the next thing I saw was some very cringe video of a renowned celebrity. I later heard the announcement from the pilot that the plane was going to take off.

The plane started to pull away from the gates and commenced taxiing towards the runway.

It only took about one minute and twenty-seven seconds for the plane to complete taxiing and enter the runway. I initiated my usual family tradition to pray when the flight took off, as my sister Andrea told me to do so, or she'd snitch on me.

- Chapter Eight -

The plane took off. I saw the panoramic view of Harmonville as we started to reach an altitude of one mile above sea level. As we started to head out of Harmonville, I randomly scrolled my TikTok page for another thirty-five seconds on my phone using onboard WiFi. I took out my tablet from my backpack - somehow my mother or Andrea did not notice it - and I opened Minecraft. I opened the realm, which I had named "Earth: The Democratic Republic of Aquilius." I examined the world, which didn't really have very much built up in it.

I got pretty tired of playing Minecraft so I swiped up to watch some football. I opened the Premier League app to find out that Manchester City (my favourite club) was playing against Manchester

United (their biggest competitor of all time). I did not expect today's football match to be a Manchester derby. My meal was served by the crew after I had watched the entire first half of the game (45 minutes).

The air hostess brought me some mac and cheese, a dish that is very popular among my friends. I put it on the tray and slowly started eating until...

The pilot announced in a panic, "Please bear with us, we have an emergency. Please put on your oxygen masks from above, there was a serious issue with navigating our way to Muscat International Airport. Everyone was bewildered by the announcement, and I heard a few people gasping out of fear. The pilot further explained that we would be making an emergency landing a few miles off San Juan, the capital of Puerto Rico. The passengers sighed in relief, despite us no longer being anywhere near Muscat, as Puerto Rico was somewhere nearby.

It only seemed to take about a couple of minutes before the plane landed on the Caribbean Sea, a few miles off the renowned capital of Puerto Rico. The floor lights on the plane's aisles turned green as the passengers continued to pray for their lives and say their final goodbyes as we landed chaotically, but safely, thanks to the genius pilot. I frantically followed the other passengers along the aisle towards the exit.

I removed my loose-fitting shirt, which I wore over a plain tee, and left it behind before going down the slides of the aircraft, as we were all instructed to do, otherwise, I may have made it difficult as I slid down the emergency exit slide.

My mother and Andrea slid before me and were now on the yellow raft, numbered "07".

- Chapter Nine -

Following my Mom and Andrea onto the emergency raft, we soon started to sail away from the wrecked plane and also further away from the coast of Puerto Rico and its capital, San Juan. We were in disbelief that we actually survived a plane crash, into water.

As we continued to sail further away from it, I checked the compass on my watch to see where we were actually headed. According to my compass, we were heading northeast.

We continued to sail further into the distance, seemingly just floating on the ocean without any guidance or direction. After such a long time in motion, I started to fall asleep, but before drifting off, I read my watch; it was 10:00 p.m. The sun had not even set yet, and I was too tired to stay awake. Eventually, I fell asleep.

- Chapter Ten -

The beaming rays of dawn roused me from my deep slumber, warming my cheeks with radiant heat. The sea was shimmering with the luminous colours of the sky. It was 8:45 a.m. and we had been floating all night. It was a relief that we were safe and had survived the first night of being stranded on a lifeboat.

In the distance, I saw some buildings and structures that looked like aircraft that seemed a few miles away. We were close to reaching land finally.

Mom was awake, trying to locate where we were on the expandable raft, and for me, happily, Andrea was still asleep like a baby.

Mom woke up Andrea by splashing water onto her, and Andrea started to scream at me, as I was known to frequently pull pranks to annoy her, and that was something that I loved to do the most.

Mom simply nudged her to stop her unwanted ranting. While on the raft, I decided to use my time wisely (by looking for food to eat on the raft), as I knew neither of us would survive for long in this misery on the raft without food, water, or even proper shelter.

My heart suddenly started to pound, and tears rolled down my face as I started to think about our situation. While I was thinking about everything that had happened, I started to look around at my surroundings, which were just plain azure water in the narrow area of the Atlantic Ocean.

Wait! I saw something peculiar: Two lands ahead of us appeared to be only a few inches apart from the distance we were from land. Of course, we were still far away from land, but at least we could see it.

Did this mean we were approaching the Strait of Gibraltar?

Another thing. Another very strange thing! I saw a rocket-looking figure in the foggy distance.

Yes!!!!!!! Finally...

We are out of here! WOO HOOO!!!

We approached the grey, angular spacecraft, which indeed did turn out to be a spacecraft. On it, 'Starbound' was written. We approached land, disembarked our trusty raft that had saved our lives, and gratefully stepped onto the landing we had awaited for so long.

As we stepped onto land, we were greeted by a crew member, a lovely woman with a light complexion, brown hair and excess lipstick - bubblegum pink in colour. She didn't explain anything to us about what we were allowed to do or what the spacecraft was even used for, and more importantly, where it was going. At this point, we had realised that we had already been through such an ordeal that this could possibly be an exciting adventure. What could go wrong, after all?

After we boarded, we were directed to our seats, 15A–C. Andrea and I played "rock, paper, scissors," which I fortunately won, so I got to sit in the window seat.

The spaceship had taken off, and the blue 14" destination board screen indicated that we were heading to Heischenbrüuke, Aquilius. It also stated that it could take forty five minutes to reach the destination. I could not believe my eyes and ears, it was an overwhelming moment, as Aquilius was the place my friends and I built in Minecraft a few days ago.

I could not comprehend what was happening to us. Was I actually dreaming about this entire thing?

Why were we chosen to take the spacecraft? Was it because we just happened to be there?

- Chapter Eleven -

Twenty-seven minutes later, we arrived at the Internationaler Flughafen Heischenbrüuke in Aquilius, so the sign read. It looked a lot like Incheon Airport in South Korea, but it looked better because there were signs at a nearby indoor water park made of vibrantly coloured concrete blocks that were conjoined with the airport, built of smooth iron blocks. Most of the signs were in the native Aquiliuite or German language. Where on earth were we? Where was this place located? I only know of this place as my creation in Minecraft. My head was heavy with these thoughts, which made me feel dizzy. I was now getting curious to explore my creation in reality... or perhaps a dream...

Leaving immigration was so hard because we could not understand what they were saying. I swear. I was so curious about this country, so I asked the immigration officer if Aquilius was part of the United Nations. The officer said "No". He said that Aquilius was instead part of MCUN. I looked up MCUN on my phone to see what it stood for.

Thankfully, we had high-speed internet. To my surprise, its full name was Minecraft United Nations.

"Aaaaahhh! WHAT??"

ONE - Minecraft was real?
TWO - We actually travelled to Minecraft.

- Chapter Twelve -

We headed towards the signage that read Line 16 (IFH AirLink) [German: Linie 16 (Flugverbindung IFH)]. I started to tremble as we took the escalator inside a rough, grey tunnel filled in with andesite to the train station. The station was built of smooth andesite and blue concrete blocks, and it resembled the railway station in Heathrow Airport Terminal 5.

I asked Mom where we were going to stay. She frowned and replied that she did not know. She spoke to the organisers who were busy working with the spacecraft. They told her that we were free to roam around and explore the block world.

The feeling was fantastic; my creation looked outstanding. I was being welcomed into surreality.

Mom checked the departure board at the train station and saw that a train would be departing at 23:34. We all ran down the escalator to find the platform.

We then headed to the high-speed platform (11), and after finding out that our train would arrive at that platform, we waited for our train. It did not take long for the announcements to call out the arrival of our train to Astragonia at about 23:30 AQST (UTC-13:00).

- Chapter Thirteen -

The grey livery train with doors that were coloured purple arrived on time. We boarded the train and were pleased by the beautiful sight of the interiors of the train, with most of it just like the interiors of an Airbus A-380. The seats were laid out in a 2-2 configuration, with the standard class seats being coloured orange and the business class seats being coloured black leather with armrests that contain cup holders; they were in a 2-1 configuration. I sat on the one-seater side, with Andrea and Mom sitting on the other.

The doors then closed and we were ready for our train journey. I heard a squeaky noise as I looked out of the window while the train began its departure from the station. I had to be honest; I was worried by the sounds that the train made and consequently started to panic.

BOOM BOOM! BOOM BOOM!...

The noise disappeared as the train sped up. I came to realise that the accelerating noise of the train originated from the engine. I felt relieved after knowing this... I saw Mom and Andrea were busy on their devices (a.k.a. gadgets). The WiFi there was indeed perfect, with little to no lag on their screens.

We exited the underground portion of the journey within the first five minutes; we were passing through a man-made ski resort made up of snow on the top of a hill, made of grass and stone blocks in the middle of a city. Then we passed a station called Madzenburg South Avenue via a vacant track powered by Redstone, and then an announcement played...

"We will shortly be arriving at Astragonia City. Please mind the gap between the train and the platform. This train terminates here. All change, please."

When I looked at Mom and Andrea's faces, they looked worried, scared and frightful because they were not familiar with the area. I was also equally curious and worried. I wondered what fate had in store for us here.

As we walked towards the doors, we saw that the station was almost completely made out of diamond. There were quite a few citizens wandering around, some slowly moving around and some, zooming around quite quickly. The elegant, rectangular-shaped citizens of this exotic country in Minecraft had respectable manners, such as queueing at the ticket counter and the machines. Their faces looked extremely pixelated, which meant that I could not calculate their ethnicity or their complexion.

Their outfits also looked simple and dull, lacking gradients on their shirts and details. Their hair looked rudimentary, as it was only composed of one colour, unlike real humans.

The world here was not as detailed as real life is, with pixelation and environmental blocks easily visible. Mom and Andrea were stunned to see this world so different from the real world.

- Chapter Fourteen -

We exited the station into Nordussia Plaza and decided to pick up a map. I decided to look around me and that was when I noticed that there were gravel pathways and no cars nearby. I also noticed that most of the buildings were built using quartz.

Mom picked up a map (it looked like a regular map, which we would normally find in a theme park). I saw Andrea daydreaming since she had not spoken a word since we arrived. Mom dragged Andrea out of her daydream as she told us which hotel we were going to stay in, looking at the map.

I was so excited about hearing which hotel we were going to, as I just wanted to crash into bed, after a long, unplanned exhausting journey, thanks to the detour we had to take here.

- Chapter Fifteen -

We entered the hotel, which looked like the letter H from its exterior, being made up of smooth quartz. It was shiny and luminous, painted with walls of white and grey in a matte style, and the kind hotel staff greeted us in such an orderly manner that we felt we were stepping onto the carpet or winning an Oscar award. Mom then told us to go and sit down on a sofa opposite the reception, as she would check us in and get the room key for us. I sat down on the grey silk sofa, away from Andrea, as I did not want to annoy her.

Mom later called us to the lift lobby, which was merely six feet wide and filled with gold. She informed us that we were going to stay on the 17th floor, which was a penthouse.

Andrea screamed 'WOW!" at the top of her voice, the moment I was about to scream with joy.

- Chapter Sixteen -

We stepped into the fancy golden lift, the appearance and technical specifications of the lift led me to believe it was a Hyundai elevator from 2022. The gleaming gold-coloured doors slid shut. Mom pressed the number 17. The floors progressed: G, 2, 3, 4, 5... in the blink of an eye.

As the floors passed, I looked around and noticed the walls of the elevator were decorated with polished limestone and gold-looking handles, garnished with emerald buttons.

Mom and Andrea appeared to be staring at the display panel which showed that the lift was currently on Level 12. I read their facial expressions. It was like they were thinking, 'Please reach faster; I want to crash in bed'.

The lift made a "ting" sound, indicating that we had reached the floor. We pushed open the door to our glamorous penthouse. All three of us were awestruck by its lavishness. Mom and Andrea's jaws' dropped. It was very late in the evening, and we were way too exhausted to scan our temporary residence.

The black-outlined white analogue clock in the room showed 3:04 a.m. as the time. We all crashed into bed, and in no time, we were in deep slumber.

- Chapter Seventeen -

I stirred in bed, as the first rays of daylight filtered through the window and eventually sat up. I stretched my arms up high to welcome the new day in my favourite world of Minecraft... I was about to get out of bed when I heard Andrea yawn loudly as she tried to wake up.

I tried to look for Mom, but she was not in bed, even though all three of us were sleeping in the same bedroom. Perhaps she was brushing her teeth. I stepped into the bathroom and sure enough, I found her there, brushing her teeth. She told me to change my clothes and find a good place to eat breakfast since room service would start at 2 p.m. and it was now too late to order breakfast as it was past 11 a.m.

Mom told us that we would leave the hotel to find a nearby restaurant. We headed out of the hotel and returned to the gravel roundabout of the Nordussia plaza.

Unexpectedly, out of excitement, Mom yelled at the top of her lungs that there were seaplanes in this country. I was astounded to see white seaplanes with yellow and blue stripes in the middle of the body on the sides of the seaplane, just like the ones in Maldives... I am not even sure if there are any water bodies on this land so I decided to look for a river or water body to find any seaplane terminals nearby.

I was wrong. There were water bodies in Aquilius, and I found a seaplane terminal.

Woohoo!!

At least I did not have to travel on a seventeen-hour flight to the Maldives just to take a ride on a seaplane!

I decided to call Mom and Andrea (who seemed

to be very bored, as she was staring into space the entire time) for the plan I had in my mind: a seaplane ride. We walked on the same gravel path to a micro-nation, which was recognized as a country called Schönbergien, as the sign read.

Engulfed in the industrial city of Glenvale - although I saw many multi-million dollar-looking block houses there, built in rich concrete, rather than warehouses or factories in that part.

Mom agreed with my plan, as did Andrea, reluctantly. We walked to the seaplane terminal, with the platforms being made up of jungle wood. There seemed to be no ticket counter, so we then headed on. We also saw a small seaplane, covered in hues of lemon yellow and sky blue, with a male pilot sitting inside of it.

It was lush green to our right, except for a railway track with a train speeding on it. To our left, I saw the Judicial District of Hoqiteng, a city adjacent to Astragonia. I opened the door of the seaplane terminal which was made of spruce wood and the seaplane pilot with a pixelated uniform asked us where we wanted to go. He had a dark complexion with a pixelated face and a tall body (2 blocks high).

Mom said, "The restaurant, please."

He winked at me while giving me a great nod.

The plane took off. I looked out of the window as it took us to the restaurant. I saw beautiful beaches made of sandblocks with a prestigious view of the city, and the block people seemed microscopic from this altitude.

During the short period, we were on the seaplane, I decided to look for the restaurant, but apparently, it was a restaurant inside a mall built from ivory-white quartz. Unbelievably, I also found the mall to be adjacent to an exuberant emerald forest canopy.

The pilot explained to us that the Vice President of the Minecraft world, Růženec Novák, had been planning a city named Redwood. He also stated that there was a major train station built alongside and above the colossal thirty-two-story mall. We arrived at the seaplane terminal, and he guided us towards the entrance of the mall. Later, we say our goodbyes and thank-you's to the pilot before entering the mall.

As soon as we entered the mall, I felt like I had entered heaven. It was so enormous and fancy that I felt like I never wanted to leave Aquilius.

Mom told us that we were going to have breakfast and then return via seaplane to explore the neighbourhood. We headed up the human-infested escalator to Level 4, where the food court was located. The mall was filled with ivory-white quartz, except for the Redstone-powered escalator. HAHA!

When we reached Level 4, the food court was to our right. It was infested with block-pixelated humans. I felt like I was trapped in an inescapable apocalypse. Nevertheless, all of us squished through the crowd to reach Aquafast, an exotic fine-dining restaurant exclusive to this land. The pilot had suggested this place for breakfast.

The waiter, dressed in a black tuxedo with a rose on his left side, smiled at us.

Mom then said, "A table for three people, please."

He said, "Sure. It's over here, to my right."

Mom saw a buffet and then told me to wait at the table with four chairs. She also said that she would give me a typical local breakfast. I couldn't believe that Aquilius even had some tasters of continental cuisine. I was sceptical about the quality of the food, but that all soon changed.

Just as I anticipated, Mom brought me a plate full of delectable items from the buffet. I was so impatient for breakfast that I even started screaming awkwardly. Thankfully, I didn't get kicked out!

After having a delicious breakfast, as we had previously arranged with our pilot, we hopped on board the same seaplane that we arrived on, and he asked us where we wanted to go.

We mentioned Hoqiteng, and he just started flying there. I sat on the opposite side of where I was sitting on the seaplane before. I noticed a few small details that I previously missed. I missed seeing the futuristic Arcane Tower with blue-stained glass cladding. I also noticed two churches, one built in wood, the other in concrete, with colourfully tinted windows. I was mesmerised by the spectacular view of the Minecraft world.

The landing was a little bumpy, but what mattered was that we arrived safely in Hoqiteng.

We thanked the pilot again for his kind and warm assistance, and we proceeded on a tour of Glensvale on foot near Hoqiteng, or by streetcar [referred to as LRT in Aquilius], where possible.

- Chapter Eighteen -

Walking to Glensvale was just too much for us (at least for me). We walked up the massive patch of grass to Glensvale (very much like Beverly Hills 2.0 in the real world). On our way, we witnessed a group of pixelated people, working together with great team effort. We saw them sharing responsibilities and building a concrete hospital together.

We continued to tour the neighbourhood and stumbled upon a school built of coloured terracotta, "Glensvale High." Wow! A Minecraft High School. We watched an airport-style screening at the entrances of the school for security reasons. We watched some pixelated pupils playing and having fun together in the school compound secured by pixelated security staff whereas other children were studying in the classrooms.

We observed the type of schooling there, saw the lovely pixelated teaching staff and learned that, of course, there had not been any school shootings there. I also, observed that there were a large number of well-functioning surveillance systems or cameras in the school.

This wonderful school inspired me to raise awareness about creating a safe and secure environment in my school. I decided that I would convince my school principal to install security cameras in our school and use security measures as in the Glensvale High School.

We walked further into the neighbourhood to discover pixelated farm animals normally crossing concrete powder roads like humans, then into an intersection, where the traffic lights were three yellow concrete blocks stacked together with item frames on each block that had concrete blocks of either red, amber, or green. The street lamps were made of andesite fences, sea lanterns, and smooth iron slabs.

Everything looked so amazing and it was all such a delight to watch.

- Chapter Nineteen -
(The Finale)

It was getting late and the sky was just the gradient of pink and orange. On our way back to the hotel, I informed Mom about how much I loved this place and that I didn't want to leave Aquilius. Andrea also agreed with my opinion.

Mom informed us that no matter how much we loved the place, as humans, we were only allowed to stay there for a certain amount of time. We were originally found in the crash site. Apparently, we had crashed in a secret place that was governed by the MCUN, Minecraft United Nations and now it was their responsibility to reach us safely home. I then started screaming, "NOOOOOOOOOOOOOOOOOOOO!!!!!!!!!!!! I don't wanna go back. NOOOOOOOOO!!!!!!!!!"

Suddenly, I felt a tight grip on my right shoulder, that woke me up. As I opened, my eyes I saw my mom trying to wake me up... She then hugged me tightly and assured me that all was well. I asked her, "Where are we?"

She replied, "Home, you have been in a deep sleep."

I was sad that it was all a dream, and happy at the same time because I could explore my Minecraft world. I longed for it to be real just like the promise that I had made to myself and that I would raise awareness about a safe and secure environment in school when I returned to school.

After a break of three weeks, I was keen to return to school today. I went to school with posters promoting peace and non-violence. I emailed the Principal, persuading her to add a tighter security system to our school with surveillance cameras and airport-style security at the entrance. I also shared information about my dream with my friends, who found it as exciting as me.

It finally came! The Principal ordered the installation of security cameras in the school, as well as airport-style checks at the entrances to the campus.

I was pleased that my wonderful experience at Aquilius enabled me to learn and apply the wonderful values of teamwork, problem-solving, creativity, and non-violence into the real world, allowing me to bring a positive change in school and make it a safe and happier place.

The End

About the Author

Gerard Adrian Menezes

Gerard is a vibrant and charismatic thirteen-year-old Dubai-based author. His favourite subjects at school are Math and Geography. Gerard loves travelling and exploring new places. In his spare time, he loves to play online games with his friends.

To follow Gerard's publishing journey, please visit,

www.youngauthoracademy.com/gerard

[Or please scan this

link with your device.]

Printed in Great Britain
by Amazon